A UNIVERSE OF STORIES

CHILDREN'S SERVICES

You read to
infinity
and beyond!

Rodgers Memorial Library
Summer Reading Program 2019

CHILDREN'S SERVICES

THIS BOOK BELONGS TO
M. COLUCI

This edition published in 1990 by Gallery Books,
an imprint of W.H. Smith Publishers, Inc.
112 Madison Avenue, New York, New York 10016

Produced for Gallery Books by Joshua Morris Publishing, Inc.,
221 Danbury Road, Wilton, CT 06897

Gallery Books are available for bulk purchase
for sales promotions and premium use.
For details write or telephone the Manager of Special Sales,
W.H. Smith Publishers, Inc., 112 Madison Avenue,
New York, New York 10016   (212) 532-6600.

Peppy

and the
Bouncy Red Ball

By Emma George
Illustrated by Carol Etow

GALLERY BOOKS
An Imprint of W. H. Smith Publishers Inc.
112 Madison Avenue
New York City 10016

One warm, spring day, Peppy and Joe went out to play. Joe took a bouncy, red ball from his pocket and showed it to Peppy.

Joe threw the ball as hard as he could.
Away went the ball, far out of sight.
"Go fetch the ball, Peppy!" yelled Joe.
So Peppy dashed after it.

But where did it go? Peppy would find it.
Peppy ALWAYS did. Sniff…

sniff…

sniff…

He found it—right next to Mrs. Duck's eggs!

But just as Peppy was about to grab the red ball, Mrs. Duck chased him away.

"QUACK, quack, quack, quack!" squawked Mrs. Duck. And she sat right on top of the bouncy, red ball.

Poor Peppy! Now what could he do!
"I know," thought Peppy. "I'll find something round. Maybe Joe won't notice that it isn't the bouncy, red ball."

Right away, Peppy found something round, and he took it straight to Joe.

But Joe said, "This isn't a ball! This is a balloon! Go fetch the ball, Peppy!"

Peppy dashed back to Mrs. Duck's nest.

He barked at her, but she was not impressed.
Mrs. Duck didn't move even one feather.

"I know," thought Peppy. "I'll find something red. Maybe Joe won't notice that it isn't the bouncy, red ball."

Soon, Peppy found something red, and he dropped it at Joe's feet.

But Joe said, "This isn't a ball! This is a mitten! Go fetch the ball, Peppy!"

Off went Peppy, once again.

This time, he saw something move in
Mrs. Duck's nest. It was just her baby ducks.
"I know," thought Peppy. "I'll find something
bouncy. Maybe Joe won't notice that it isn't the
bouncy, red ball."

Soon, Peppy found something bouncy, and
it bounced all the way back with him to Joe.
"Yikes!" yelled Joe. "This isn't a ball. This
is a frog! I'll have to find that ball myself."

Off marched Joe, across the meadow.

Soon he was looking right into Mrs. Duck's nest. But where was Mrs. Duck? And where were all her eggs? Why, the only thing left was...

…the bouncy, red ball!

"I knew I could find it!" cried Joe.

He picked up the ball, and guess what he did with it? He threw that ball as far as he could.

Away went the ball, far out of sight.

"Fetch the ball, Peppy!" yelled Joe.

Off dashed Peppy. This time he'd get it. This time he really would!

"Oh, no!" thought Peppy.
"Here we go again!"